RSPCA

Puppy Gets Stuck

The Royal Society for the Prevention of Cruelty to Animals is the UK's largest animal charity. They rescue, look after and rehome hundreds of thousands of animals each year in England and Wales. They also offer advice on caring for all animals and campaign to change laws that will protect them. Their work relies on your support, and buying this book helps them save animals' lives.

www.rspca.org.uk

RSPCA

Puppy Gets Stuck

By Sue Mongredien
Illustrated by Jon Davis

SCHOLASTIC

First published in the UK in 2013 by Scholastic Children's Books
An imprint of Scholastic Ltd
Euston House, 24 Eversholt Street
London, NW1 1DB, UK
Registered office: Westfield Road, Southam, Warwickshire, CV47 0RA
SCHOLASTIC and associated logos are trademarks
and/or registered trademarks of Scholastic Inc.

ISBN 978 1407 13322 5

A CIP catalogue record for this book is available
from the British Library.

Printed and bound by CPI Group (UK) Ltd, Croydon, CR0 4YY
Papers used by Scholastic Children's Books are made
from wood grown in sustainable forests.

7 9 10 8

This is a work of fiction. Names, characters, places,
incidents and dialogues are products of the author's imagination
or are used fictitiously. Any resemblance to actual people,
living or dead, events or locales is entirely coincidental.

www.scholastic.co.uk/zone

1

"Hello, Pickle!" It was Friday afternoon, and nine-year-old Emily Wilson had run straight out of school and down the drive to the gates. There was her gorgeous spaniel puppy waiting for her, his feathery white tail beating with delight, his huge brown eyes round and bright as he saw her coming.

Woof! he went, tugging at the lead as if he just couldn't wait another second to be with her. *Woof, woof!*

Dumping her school bag on the grass, Emily crouched down and threw

her arms around her puppy, making an enormous fuss of him. She cuddled him and fluffed up his soft brown and white fur and scratched him behind his long silky ears. Pickle, meanwhile, kept licking her face, his wet black nose cold against her cheek, his tail wagging even faster. He really was the cutest puppy *ever*, and her best friend in the whole world.

"Hello to you too, Em," came Mum's amused voice, and Emily looked up with a smile to see her there with Jack, Emily's brother, who was five.

"Hi, Mum. Hi, Jack," Emily said, getting up and hugging her mum. "Can I take Pickle's lead now?"

"Of course," Mum said. "I thought we could go to Albany Woods for a walk."

"Yay!" cheered Jack, and Pickle immediately started barking and leaping around at the word "walk" as if he agreed.

Emily grinned. "You know what *that* word means, don't you?" She laughed, reaching down to pat his side. "Your favourite word of all!"

"I think he's learned some new favourite words today," Mum said as they set off down the road. "Cheese straws."

Pickle woofed immediately.

"What do you mean?" asked Emily.

"I baked some cheese straws this afternoon," Mum explained, "and had just left them cooling on the table when the doorbell rang. . ."

"Uh-oh." Emily laughed. She had a pretty good idea of how this story might go.

"And guess who scrambled up to the table while I went to answer the door . . . and ate *four* of them?" Mum finished.

Pickle gave another woof as if he were proudly saying, *Me! I did it! That's how clever I am!* and Emily giggled. "Pickle by name, pickle by nature," she said affectionately, watching as he stopped to sniff a lamp post.

Jack looked worried. "Are there any cheese straws left?" he asked.

Mum ruffled his hair. "There are plenty left," she said, "and they're safely in a tin now, well out of reach of greedy pups. Apart from these two, which I brought along just in case there are any hungry children. . ."

"Me!" cried Jack at once.

"Thanks, Mum," said Emily, munching hers. She gave the lead a gentle tug. "Come on, Pickle, enough sniffing." He was so inquisitive that he liked to stop and smell *everything*: a nettle, the wall, a piece of litter. . . He'd often swerve right in front of Emily's legs to get to a particularly exciting gateway or hedge, and had nearly tripped her up several times in his eagerness.

Emily didn't mind. Pickle was so funny and lovely, she could forgive him anything. Ever since she'd first seen him, when they'd gone to the rehoming centre on her ninth birthday, she had been totally smitten. Back then, he'd been no more than a handful of brown and white fur with a soft round tummy and a fluffy tail. Emily's heart had simply melted when he'd gambolled over to her with a little yip of excitement, his big round eyes shining. "This one's my favourite," she'd said, reaching down to scoop him up. "Look, Mum!"

"I think he's chosen you, too," Mum had said laughing as Pickle poked out a teeny pink tongue and licked Emily's cheek.

They'd had to wait eight weeks – the longest eight weeks of Emily's life! – before the puppies were old enough to leave their mum, a sweet-natured rescue dog who was going to a new home, too. At last Emily had been able to collect Pickle, and he'd quickly become part of the family. He was nearly six months old now, and his tiny, stumpy legs had grown longer, as had his feathery tail. Emily could hardly remember what life had been like before he'd come to live with them. Having Pickle made everything much more fun, that was for sure.

"Good boy," Emily said encouragingly as he trotted along beside her. "That's it – heel!"

She and Dad had just started taking Pickle to puppy training classes, and she was trying to teach him different commands. He'd been to two lessons so far, although both had been a bit of a disaster. During the first one, Pickle had just wanted to play with all the other puppies. He was such a friendly little dog, he had kept scampering up to them whenever he'd had the chance, sniffing them and cheerfully waving his tail as if to say hello. He'd also done quite a lot of excited barking. Oh yes, and then he'd weed on the floor right at the end. . .

Luckily, the training lady had just smiled. "I've seen it all before," she'd said, passing Dad a mop. "And let's face it . . . it could have been worse."

So far Pickle had learned to sit (with a bit of help – you had to push his bottom down to remind him), and stay (for about five whole seconds) and walk to heel. Recently, Emily had tried to teach him to get into his basket, too, although he tended to jump in and then jump straight out again, his tail wagging proudly as if to say, *There – I did it. What game shall we play now?*

Once they reached the woods, Emily unclipped Pickle's lead. She could always feel him trembling with excitement whenever she let him off it. As soon as he was free this time, he gave a big happy woof and bounded down the track, his floppy ears flying out to the sides like furry brown wings. He sniffed at every tree, put his head down a rabbit hole and nosed eagerly through the long grass like an intrepid explorer on an expedition.

Emily and Jack ran beside him while Mum walked behind with their school bags. Now that Pickle's legs were longer, he could go quite fast, especially when he saw a squirrel up ahead on the path. Barking non-stop, he charged breathlessly towards the creature – which promptly shot straight up the nearest tree, its bushy tail twitching.

Emily laughed. "Oh, Pickle," she said, as he put his front paws against the tree trunk and yapped a great long message to the squirrel. "Come on," she called, "leave the poor thing alone."

It was a sunny spring day and the dappled light shone between the leafy branches of the trees. Daffodils bobbed their heads in a breeze, and the air felt warm against Emily's face. Mum suggested that they go further into the woods than usual as it was such a lovely day, and everyone – especially Pickle – thought that this was a very good idea.

They rounded the corner, and Emily saw that one of the large natural ponds in this part of the wood was covered with bright green duckweed. Pickle noticed it too, and rushed off to investigate. Unfortunately, he seemed to think the green duckweed was ordinary grass and ran cheerfully on to it . . . and in the very next moment, the "grass" gave way and he splashed straight into the water!

Emily gasped. "Pickle!" she cried, rushing over at once. The little puppy gave a yip of surprise as he found himself in the cold pond, and had to paddle his front paws to keep afloat. He was probably wondering how the grass had turned into water.

"He's swimming," Jack shouted, laughing. "Keep going, Pickle, you might get your five-metre badge!"

Emily laughed too. Pickle seemed to be rather enjoying himself, now that he'd got over the shock of cold water, and was swimming around very splashily. "Come on, boy, over here," she called, bending over a little and patting her thighs encouragingly. "Come to me, that's it."

She reached out her hand and as soon as he'd paddled near enough, she grabbed his collar and hauled him out of the water.

Covered with duckweed and mud, Pickle looked completely bedraggled. He smelled absolutely terrible, too.

"Pickle Wilson, what are you like?" Emily groaned. "Look at him, Mum."

"Poo!" Jack said, holding his nose. "Pickle pongs."

"It's not his fault," Emily said loyally. "Is it, boy? He. . . Aargh!" She leaped back as Pickle chose that very moment to give himself a thorough shake, spraying Emily with stinky mud from head to foot.

"Yuck!" she shrieked, wiping a strand of duckweed from her face. Pickle wagged his tail as if he'd just been very helpful, and Emily found herself giggling. You really couldn't be cross with a puppy like Pickle!

Jack burst out laughing, and Mum looked as if she was trying not to chuckle too. "Oh dear," she said. "What a mucky pup — and what a mucky daughter! I hope you two won't get too cold now you're so wet. Perhaps we'd better head back."

Emily agreed. "Let's put you on the lead, Pickle," she said, clipping it safely on to his collar. "I think that's enough exploring for one day, don't you? We don't want you getting into another pickle!"

Woof! Pickle agreed, wagging his muddy tail.

They set off towards home, Pickle's fur slowly drying in the sunshine. As they passed their neighbours' house they saw that Mr and Mrs Turner were in their front garden, pulling up some weeds.

Mr Turner looked up and smiled when he saw them. "Goodness me, Pickle, what *have* you been up to?" he asked.

Mrs Turner's eyes twinkled. "It looks like somebody will be going straight into the bath when you get home," she said, laughing.

Mum shook her head. "I'm tempted to put the pair of them in together," she joked. "I'm not sure who's the muddiest, Emily or the dog!"

Once they were back inside, Emily quickly changed out of her muddy clothes and helped Mum fill the bath for Pickle, who wasn't very happy about being washed at all. Despite Emily's best

efforts, he kept trying to clamber out, his claws uselessly scrabbling at the side. Water and the bubbles from his special doggy shampoo went *everywhere*, and soon Emily and Mum were drenched, too.

Afterwards, Emily dried Pickle in a big fluffy towel and brushed the tangles out of his fur. "There," she said when it shone once more. "You're as good as new."

Once Pickle had eaten his tea, he seemed so tired that he barely had the energy to move. Instead of making the short journey to his basket, he curled up on the floor by his food bowl and closed his eyes.

Emily smiled as his head sank dreamily on to his front paws. "Pickle! Get in your basket." she reminded him in the sing-song voice she always tried to use when giving him commands.

Pickle opened one eye and peered groggily at her.

"Good boy, Pickle, get in your basket," Emily coaxed.

Pickle was so sleepy he could hardly walk, but he obediently staggered to his feet and trotted over to his basket. He flopped into it, gave a deep sigh of relief, tucked his nose under his favourite cuddly bear, then promptly fell straight back to sleep. Within seconds he was snoring.

Emily stroked his soft fur. "What a good boy," she told him, gently resting her head on his sleeping body and listening to his heartbeat. "I hope you have a lovely dream about chasing squirrels. Sleep well . . . and let's have another adventure tomorrow."

2

Emily had always enjoyed weekends, but ever since Pickle had joined the family, she loved them even more. Two whole days of puppy play! She couldn't think of anything nicer. Even better, her friend Chloe was coming over for the morning, too.

Emily scrambled out of bed and pulled on her dressing gown, then went downstairs to see her pup. He had obviously been exploring the shoe basket by the back door, because he'd pulled all the shoes out of it and was now having a fight with one of Dad's slippers. He growled with excitement as he chewed it with his sharp little teeth and dragged it around the kitchen to show it who was boss.

"Hey, you," Emily said, hurrying over. "Don't let Dad see you doing that, you monkey." Just the week before, Pickle had chewed right through the toes of one of Mum's designer shoes. He'd been in deep disgrace for that. "Give it, Pickle. Drop!"

Pickle ignored her and shook the slipper around some more, still growling softly at it from between his teeth. Why on earth would he want to drop this new toy, which smelled so interesting?

"Come on, Pickle," Emily coaxed, pulling gently on the slipper. "Drop, I said. Drop it!"

But Pickle still wouldn't drop it. He was having too much fun!

"How about playing with Bear instead?" Emily offered, picking up his favourite cuddly toy from his basket. But even the blue bear – much chewed and loved – didn't seem as exciting as Dad's slipper today.

It was only when Emily tipped some puppy food into his bowl that Pickle finally decided that OK, perhaps the slipper *wasn't* actually the tastiest thing after all, and dropped it on the floor.

Emily examined the slipper while Pickle ate his breakfast. Uh-oh. It was wet and slobbery and there were toothmarks in the sole. Dad wouldn't be very happy about *that*. She did her best to dry it with a towel and attempted to press flat some of the toothmarks, but it still didn't look quite right. Hmm. She just hoped Dad would be too bleary-eyed that morning to notice.

Emily put the slipper back in the shoe basket along with all the others that Pickle had cheekily pulled out. Then, after a moment's thought, she draped the towel over the top of the basket. If Pickle couldn't actually *see* the shoes, she thought, maybe he wouldn't realize they were still inside. Genius!

Pickle glanced up at her while he ate, and she ruffled his fur, feeling pleased with her idea. Then she poured herself some cereal and a glass of milk and sat down at the table.

"Morning," said Dad, coming into the kitchen wearing his dressing gown. He raised an eyebrow as he noticed what she had done to the basket of shoes. "Emily," he began, "why. . .?"

He broke off in the next moment. Breakfast finished, Pickle had romped straight back over to the shoe basket with an excited bark. He nosed eagerly under the towel for a few moments before re-emerging with Dad's slipper in his mouth and the towel now dangling on his head. Then he gave a muffled woof, ran over to Emily and dropped the slipper at her feet, wagging his tail. It was as if he were saying, *Found it! Even with that towel! You can't fool me!*

Emily and Dad laughed and laughed. "You rascal," Dad said affectionately, reaching down and taking the towel off Pickle's head. "Honestly, what a daft dog!"

Pickle began bounding back and forth from the shoe basket, barking and wagging his tail and looking *very* proud of himself.

"Here we go again," Emily groaned as Pickle pulled out one of Jack's trainers with great enthusiasm and dumped it on the floor. Then out came the other trainer. Then one of Emily's red wellies, which he had to heave and heave at. Emily couldn't help giggling. Pickle was unstoppable!

"Well, at least I know what my first job of the day is going to be," Dad said as he filled the kettle at the sink. "Making a lid for the shoe basket – so that it's puppy-proof!"

Later that morning, Emily's best friend Chloe came round to play. It was a sunny day, so she and Emily decided to go out into the garden, closely followed by Pickle, who began nosing his red ball around the lawn. Every now and then he would bring it over to Emily, who threw it for him to chase after and fetch.

Meanwhile, the girls began making a "fairy house" together in one of the flower beds. Emily collected some just-fallen red tulip petals, which made a perfect silky bed, Chloe picked a dandelion flower to use as a pillow, and they both found a few soft pieces of moss that could be velvety fairy cushions.

"It looks great," Emily said, sitting back to admire it. "Now, what could we use to make a table and chair?"

Before they could start looking for anything, though, Pickle came rushing along with his ball and trampled clumsily right through the fairy house to get to Emily's side.

"Oh no!" cried Chloe in dismay as his paws broke the tulip-petal bed. "It's ruined."

"Pickle!" Emily groaned, feeling disappointed.

Hearing her tone of voice, Pickle's tail drooped and his big brown eyes turned anxious and uncertain. He stood looking at Emily, his head on one side, and gave a little whine.

Emily reached out to pat him. "Oh, it's all right, boy, I'm not cross," she said after a moment. "You didn't know, did you?"

He licked her face and gave a small woof as if to say sorry, and Emily pulled him close for a cuddle. "He's still only a baby," she said to Chloe. "Maybe we should think of something else to do."

Just then Mum came out with some

chocolate brownies and glasses of lemon squash, so the girls had a little picnic on the lawn while they thought. Then Emily had an idea. "Let's set up camp out here," she suggested. "We could make a tent out of a sheet, and use some chairs and things to hold it up. What do you think?"

"Brilliant," Chloe agreed at once.

The girls set to work. Mum let them carry two of the kitchen chairs outside and gave them an old sheet to drape across the top to make a roof. Dad brought out the clothes rack that they sometimes used to dry clothes, and they hung an old towel over it to make a third wall to their shelter. The sheet sagged in the middle, until Chloe had the clever idea of using pegs off the washing line to clip it more securely to the rack. The camp was coming together!

Mrs Turner was in the garden next door, watering her vegetables. She waved when she saw the girls. "Building an extension, are we?" she said with a smile, looking over the fence at their tent.

"Yes," Emily replied proudly. "It's our new secret hideout."

She and Chloe crawled inside. "We could be cave girls," Chloe suggested. "Sheltering in our cave from the wolves outside."

"Ooh, yes," Emily said. Then she giggled as a little brown face poked inquisitively around the doorway. She should have known he wouldn't be able to resist exploring the tent for long. "Oh no!" she cried, pointing dramatically. "A wolf's coming into our cave! Help!"

She and Chloe clutched each other, squealing and pretending to be scared. The "wolf" gave a big woof and bounded into the tent, wagging his tail and jumping at the girls as if trying to join in the game.

"Help!" Chloe cried. "I'm being licked to death by a wolf."

"Don't eat us, wolf," Emily giggled,

rolling back on to the grass. "We beg you – spare our lives!"

The wolf seemed to like the tent. Once he'd spared the girls' lives – just – he sniffed at every corner of it, his nose twitching. Then he barked cheerfully and trotted out again, his tail wagging excitedly.

"Hey, maybe we could get a rug or something to lie on next," Chloe said, looking around when Pickle had gone. "That would make it even cosier in here."

"Good thinking," Emily said. "Let's go up to my bedroom and see what we can find."

The two friends went inside the house to look for suitable bits and bobs. Mum was just about to drop Jack off at a friend's birthday party but gave them a second old sheet to use as their carpet before she left. Then the girls collected up an armful of soft pillows, a board game to play and some books. "We can stay in our tent all day," Emily said happily.

Chloe picked up a packet of felt-tips. "Let's draw some pictures and stick them to the walls, too," she suggested. "It'll be the perfect girls' hang-out."

But when they returned to the garden, they saw that their camp wasn't looking quite as good as before. It certainly wasn't a perfect girls' hang-out! The chairs had been tipped over, and the sheet had been dragged across the lawn and now had muddy paw prints all over it. Pickle's eyes were wild as he tugged at it with his teeth.

"Oh no," Chloe exclaimed. "Not again!"

Emily felt fed up, too. "Pickle, that was

naughty," she told him, trying to prise the sheet from his mouth. "You spoiled our tent." She pulled at the sheet but Pickle seemed to think this was an exciting new game and wouldn't let go. "Give," Emily said crossly. "Give!"

She gave the sheet another pull, harder this time . . . and then they heard a loud *rrrrrrip* as it tore. "Pickle," Emily said, letting go before the tear grew even bigger. "*Now* look what you've done!"

Dad came outside to see what all the noise was about. "Oh dear," he said when he saw the wreckage. "Did someone call the tent-demolition squad or is this the work of young master Pickle?"

Emily's cheeks felt hot. "That's the second game of ours he's ruined, Dad!" she complained. "Now we'll have to start all over again."

Dad put a hand on her shoulder. "He didn't mean to ruin anything," he reminded Emily. "He's still young and mischievous, that's all. I know it's annoying, but he was only playing."

Sensing he was in his mistress's bad books, Pickle finally dropped the sheet and walked over to Emily, pressing his head against her bare legs and giving a little whine. He wagged his tail hopefully, as if trying to make friends.

Emily gave a sigh, then crouched down and hugged him. Dad was right. "I know you didn't mean to ruin our tent," she said, patting him gently. "But sometimes you're a pest, Pickle-pops."

"Tell you what," Dad said. "Once your mum's home again I'll take him out on a long w-a-l-k." He spelled out the word so that Pickle wouldn't understand and start going bonkers with excitement. "And then you'll have a chance to set up your camp properly again. I'll even give you a hand rebuilding the tent before I go. What do you think?"

"Thanks, Dad," Emily replied, just as Chloe said, "Yes, please."

"Right," Dad said. "Well, first things first, let's get matey-boy inside." He scooped up Pickle, who licked his face. "Then we'll get started. Don't worry, girls. It'll be the best tent ever, if I've got anything to do with it."

3

The rest of the morning was great
fun. True to his word, Dad helped the
girls build a really cool new tent, and
then they enjoyed making it cosy and
comfortable inside. Mum came back
from dropping off Jack, and Dad took
Pickle for a walk in the woods, so
Emily and Chloe were left in peace
and quiet. They lay on their tummies in
the tent, drawing pictures and using safety
pins to attach them to the inside of the
sheet-wall. "We're not cave girls any
more," Chloe said with a grin. "We're

famous artists, and this is our gallery."

Emily looked at her picture. She was drawing Pickle with a bone in his mouth standing in a big flowery meadow. "I'll probably sell this for a million pounds," she declared, making his tail a bit fluffier. "*If* I decide to sell it, that is."

Chloe giggled. "People will queue for miles to see our work," she went on dreamily, adding seagulls to the beach picture she was working on. "We'll be so famous we'll never have to go to school again. . ."

"Lunch time!" called Mum.

The girls smiled at each other and went into the kitchen, where Mum was laying plates of food on the table. She must have stopped at the bakery on the way home, Emily realized, because there were warm sausage rolls and gingerbread men decorated with chocolate icing. It all smelled delicious.

"Can we have lunch in our tent, please?" Emily asked hopefully.

"Of course," Mum said. "If you find a tray, Em, we can load it up with goodies."

The girls helped themselves to a sausage roll and a gingerbread man, as well as a juicy red apple each and a handful of fat green grapes to share. Then Mum poured them glasses of water with clinking ice cubes and helped carry everything out to the tent.

"Perfect," Chloe said as they leaned back on their pillows, munching happily.

"Yep," Emily agreed. She never would have admitted it out loud, but it was actually sort of nice to have Pickle out of the way for a change while they enjoyed their game. As much as she loved him, sometimes she wanted to play with Chloe, just the two of them, without Pickle joining in.

The girls finished lunch and took their plates back inside, then started a new game, climbing up into the cherry tree and pretending it was a boat. It was cool and breezy up there, and the pink blossom smelled beautiful.

Jack came home after a while — a neighbour had brought him back from the party — and the girls made him jump by dropping petals on his head when he came out to look for them. "Hey!" he shouted when he realized what was happening. He shook the petals from his hair and the girls nearly fell out of the branches giggling.

Emily grinned. "I hope Pickle's home soon," she said. "Imagine his face when he sees us up here. He'll be so confused that I'm not down on the ground with him."

Just as she said these words she heard Dad's voice from inside the house. They were back!

"Pickle!" Emily called from the tree, expecting him to come charging outside to find her. She smiled to herself as she pictured him sniffing all around the garden trying to spot her and Chloe.

But Pickle didn't appear. That was strange. Then Emily realized how quickly Dad was talking to Mum inside. His voice sounded urgent and worried. What was going on?

"Shall we get down now?" Chloe asked.

"Wait," Emily said. "Listen." She kept still, trying to hear what Dad was saying.

"And he hasn't come back here?" he was asking Mum. "Oh no. I was hoping he might have found his way home. . ."

Emily realized she was gripping the branch so hard her knuckles had turned white. What was Dad talking about? *I was hoping he might have found his way home*, he'd said. Surely he didn't mean. . .

"Back in a minute," she muttered to Chloe and scrambled down from the tree, her heart beating faster than usual. *No*, she told herself. *Don't be silly, Em.* Of course Pickle was with Dad. Where else would he be? She must have heard wrong. "Pickle!" she called again, her voice sounding shrill. "Where are you, boy?"

She ran into the kitchen, only to see her parents both looking anxious.

"Oh, Em. . ." her dad began, his mouth twisting in a strange, tense sort of way.

"What? What's happened? Where is he?" Emily said, her words tumbling over one another as she spoke. "Where's Pickle?"

Jack and Chloe followed, and there was an awful moment as they all waited for Dad to reply. He passed a hand through his hair, looking awkward. "I'm really sorry," he said at last. "I let him off the lead for a while and he must have got lost. I called and called but he didn't

come back." He shrugged. "I was hoping
he'd be here. I thought he might have
found his own way home, but. . ."

Emily swallowed. "He isn't here," she
said. Her voice sounded weird, as if it
was coming from far away, and her heart
seemed to pound even harder. Her legs
felt numb and wobbly as if they might
give way at any moment. "He must still
be out there somewhere."

Jack looked worried. "But *where*?" he cried. "Where *is* he?"

Mum put her arm around him. "We'll all go and look for him," she said. "He can't have gone far. You know what he's like – he's probably just gone off exploring and got himself lost."

"But what if. . .?" Emily began. Her mind was already spinning with a thousand terrible "what ifs". What if he'd wandered into a road and been hit by a car? What if he'd hurt himself and was lying all alone in the woods? And what if . . . what if somebody thought he didn't have an owner and had taken him home with *them*? She swallowed, trying to clear her head of such awful thoughts.

"We'll find him," Dad said as if he could read her mind. "I promise."

"Let's retrace your steps through the woods," Mum suggested to Dad. "We can drop Chloe off on the way." She gave Chloe an apologetic smile. "Sorry, love. I'll give your mum a quick call. I'm sure she'll understand."

"It's fine," Chloe said. She squeezed Emily's hand. "I can phone around when I get home and ask other people to look out for him," she suggested. "Poor little Pickle! I wonder where he is?"

They locked the back door and went out of the front together. Mum dialled Chloe's parents on her mobile as they hurried down the road.

Emily felt as if she was in a dream. It seemed so wrong, all of them walking down the road together without Pickle. She kept expecting to feel him brushing against her legs, or hear him bark. Where was he? All she could think about was how she'd called him a pest for knocking down the camp. Her cheeks burned as she remembered how she hadn't even missed him while he'd been out with Dad. In fact, she'd enjoyed playing with Chloe without him interrupting.

"I hope we find him soon," she said in a small voice. "I hope he's not scared."

"Honestly, darling, I'm sure he's absolutely fine," Mum said as they neared Chloe's street. "Try not to worry. He's probably having a wonderful time chasing a squirrel somewhere. We'll find him."

Emily managed a small smile, imagining Pickle lolloping joyfully after every last squirrel, rabbit and mouse that lived in the woods. Mum was right – chances were he was having the time of his life.

"I hope so," she replied shakily.

They dropped Chloe off and she hugged Emily goodbye. "I'll tell our neighbours," she said, "and phone everyone I can think of. Let me know when you find him, won't you?"

"I will," Emily said. "Thanks, Clo." She tried to smile but as soon as they walked away from Chloe's house, her optimism faltered. Poor Pickle. What if she'd really upset him, telling him off for spoiling their tent? He might have run away on purpose. Maybe he was wishing he had a nicer owner, one who always let him join in with her games.

Emily sniffed at the thought. It was too awful to bear. She could feel her bottom lip start to wobble – always a sign that she was close to tears. "Mum," she said quietly as they carried on down the road.

"What if Pickle doesn't *want* to be found? What if he doesn't want to live with us any more?"

4

Mum put her arms around Emily at once. "Nonsense," she said firmly. "Don't even *think* that. I've never seen a happier puppy than Pickle – and that's because of the caring way you look after him. He adores you, Em. He absolutely loves you! If anyone can help find him, it's you, OK?"

Emily felt a bit better. She blew her nose and nodded. "OK," she said. "And I *will* find him." *And when I do*, she thought to herself, *I'll make the biggest fuss of him ever. I'll never call him a pest again!*

They retraced Dad's steps through the woods and around the fields and farmland, calling Pickle's name every few minutes.

They passed quite a few dogwalkers that Emily recognized, and the family stopped each time to ask if anyone had seen Pickle. Nobody had, but they all took a note of Mum's mobile number and promised to call if they saw him. "We lost Shelley once," one lady said, patting her Labrador as she spoke. "Didn't find her for hours, so I know how you must be feeling. At least there aren't any busy roads around here. He's probably just wandered off – it happens so easily with a puppy."

Emily felt comforted by the lady's words. "Where did you find Shelley in the end?" she asked.

"Down near Fletchers' Farm," the lady said. "She was playing with the farm dogs as if she didn't have a care in the world, when I'd been tearing my hair out with worry." She smiled. "I was so relieved, I couldn't be cross. Anyway, I won't keep you. I hope you find your puppy – I'll certainly keep an eye out for him."

They thanked the lady and went on their way. "I hope Pickle's playing with some other dogs," Jack mumbled sadly.

"Me too," Emily said. Poor Jack looked

almost as upset as she'd been feeling. "I bet he is," she said, trying to sound more confident for his sake. "You know how friendly he is. Even at the dog training classes, he was trying to make friends with all the other puppies, wasn't he, Dad?"

"He was," Dad agreed. "And hopefully if he *is* with another dog, the owners will give us a ring and let us know. Our phone number's on his collar, remember. I'm sure any dog owner will look after him until we can go and pick him up. We'd do the same if we found a lost puppy, wouldn't we?"

"Yes," Emily agreed. "We would." She was feeling more positive by the minute. They would find Pickle soon, she knew it. They had to!

Two hours later, they had walked for

miles and Jack was complaining that his feet hurt. Emily's feet were getting tired and sore too, but she couldn't bring herself to say so.

"I think we should turn back," Mum said eventually. "It's starting to get cold, and it'll be dark before long. And you never know, somebody might have left a message on our home phone."

Dad agreed. "Once we're back, we can ring around the local farms," he added. "Ask them to check their outbuildings, just in case Pickle has been accidentally shut in a barn or shed."

"He might have found his way home," Emily said hopefully. "He could be waiting for us on the doorstep!" It was just the sort of thing Pickle would do, she thought, and that would explain why they hadn't found him in the woods.

She imagined herself running down the road towards him, laughing with relief. *THERE you are!* she would say as he bounded up to meet her. *You found your own way back, did you? What a clever little puppy!*

As they walked into their village and came to their road at last, Emily forgot all about her aching legs and feet and began to run. She was so sure that Pickle would be there waiting for her, wagging his feathery tail and barking with joy to see her. He had to be! "Pickle! Pickle!" she yelled. "We're back!"

She sped past Mr and Mrs Turner, who were unloading some shopping bags from their little blue car, and charged up the path to their house. "Pickle, are you there?" she called, her voice catching on the words as she stared into every corner

of the front garden. *Please be here*, she thought desperately. *Please, please have come home, Pickle!*

Silence greeted her words. There was no joyful bark, no scuffle of paws. Emily's shoulders fell as bitter disappointment rushed through her.

"Is everything all right, dear?" Mrs Turner called over in concern.

Tears brimmed in Emily's eyes. She'd tried so hard not to cry ever since Pickle had gone missing, but she couldn't hold back any more. "We've lost Pickle," she said as the first tears rolled down her cheeks. "We've been calling and calling for hours, but we can't find him anywhere."

"Oh lovey," said Mrs Turner, putting her shopping down and coming over to hug Emily. Mum, Dad and Jack walked up the path then, too.

"Isn't he here?" Jack asked, sounding disappointed.

Emily shook her head. "No," she replied in a muffled voice, still in Mrs Turner's arms.

"Well, we haven't seen him," Mrs Turner said, "and we've been out and about all afternoon. I know we would have noticed if he'd been scampering around the village. Have you tried phoning the local vets in case anyone has found him and taken him there?"

Mr Turner had come over to join them. "You could try the RSPCA, too. They've got a centre not far from here," he suggested.

"Thanks, we will," Mum said. She stroked Emily's hair. "Don't fret. He's got to be somewhere."

★

They went inside and checked the answerphone for messages. Nobody had left one, other than Chloe asking if there was any news.

Dad made a few phone calls while Mum started cooking dinner. The house felt so empty and quiet without Pickle. Every room Emily went into reminded her of him: his spare lead in the hall, his toys scattered around the living room, his food bowl and bed in the kitchen. She kept expecting him to come bursting in, racing over to her barking, his tail wagging non-stop as he licked her face. But he didn't.

Emily went over to Pickle's basket and knelt beside it for a moment, looking at her puppy's blanket and his favourite cuddly bear, which was lying in there as always. She remembered how, just the

day before, she'd been there coaxing him
to "Get in your basket!" and how he'd
stumbled sleepily across the room to
clamber inside. He was so sweet when
he was tired.

With a lump in her throat, she found
herself stroking the soft fleecy lining of
the basket, wishing that Pickle was curled
up in there tonight, snoring his cute
doggy snores again.

She sat back on her heels and sighed. If only she hadn't been so keen for Dad to take him out on a long walk, Pickle would be here now. If only she'd suggested that she and Chloe went on the walk, too, she could have kept a closer eye on him!

She gave a little sob, and Mum glanced over at her. "Oh, darling, don't cry," she said gently. "I know you're worried, but I'm sure we'll get him back soon. Someone will find him, even if we didn't. Don't lose hope!"

Emily nodded, wiping her eyes. She mustn't give up on finding Pickle. And she shouldn't sit around feeling sorry for herself while he was still out there, all on his own. He was counting on her to find him and she wouldn't let her best friend down!

Dad came into the room just then.

"I've left messages with all the farmers, and tried the local vets and the RSPCA, too," he said. "I figured the more people who know about him the better."

"Thanks, Dad," Emily said. His words had given her an idea, and she got to her feet.

"Can I go up and down our road, asking people if they've seen Pickle?" she begged her parents. There were only fifteen or so houses on the road and Emily knew everyone who lived there.

Mum looked up from chopping onions. "Good idea," she said. "Come straight back afterwards, though, won't you, because dinner will be ready at six. And don't cross the road without being very careful."

"OK," Emily said. They were lucky enough to live on a quiet street with hardly any traffic, but she knew to always stop and check.

"Ask people if they'd mind looking in their garages and sheds, too," Dad suggested. "He's such an inquisitive little fella, he might have found his way in somewhere and got trapped."

"OK," Emily said again. "I won't be long."

She went out into the street and began knocking on her neighbours' doors. As soon as she said Pickle was lost, everyone was full of concern. "Let me know if he's still not back tomorrow and you want help looking," said Mr Warburton at number twelve.

"I'll keep an eye out when we walk Buster later on," promised Mrs Jackson at number ten. "If he's anywhere around here, Buster will sniff him out, don't you worry."

"I'll tell everyone down at the pub to watch out for him," said Lizzie Miles at number six. She worked as a waitress in The Red Lion on Saturday nights, and was just heading off there when Emily knocked.

"Thanks," Emily said – to Lizzie and Mrs Jackson and Mr Warburton, and to everyone else who kindly offered to help. Although he was only a little pup, Pickle was well loved in the village. Everyone seemed sorry to hear he'd gone missing.

Emily glanced at her watch and saw that it was almost six o'clock, so she trudged back home, hoping there might be good news waiting for her. Maybe somebody had phoned to say they'd found him. Maybe right now, Dad was grabbing the car keys, about to set off and collect him.

She ran the last few steps home with her fingers crossed. *Hang on, Pickle,* she murmured under her breath. *We'll have you home soon — I promise.*

5

Everyone was quiet as they ate dinner that evening. The phone rang and Emily nearly knocked over her chair rushing to answer it, but it was only Grandma calling for a chat. Then, as they were halfway

through pudding, the doorbell chimed and once again Emily bolted from her seat to answer it, with hopeful visions of one of their neighbours standing there with Pickle in their arms. It was just one of Dad's friends, though, stopping by to talk about the game of golf they'd arranged later in the week.

"Maybe we should have one last look around the village," Emily suggested as she helped Dad load the dishwasher with their plates and cutlery.

Dad shook his head. "It's getting dark now, love," he replied. "Let's set out in the morning and look again then."

Emily's shoulders drooped. "I just hate the thought of him being somewhere out there, all on his own," she said, gazing into the garden. "He'll be so scared and cold."

Dad put an arm around her. "He's a clever little pup remember," he said comfortingly. "I bet he's found somewhere really cosy to sleep, and is all curled up, his nose tucked in his paws, while he dreams about the adventures he's had. And tomorrow morning, first thing, we'll go out looking again – all day if we have to. We won't stop looking until we've found him, all right?"

Emily nodded. "All right," she agreed.

A bit later, Mum helped Emily clear up the tent she and Chloe had made in the garden. As Emily carried in their drawings, the picture she'd drawn of Pickle with the bone in his mouth gave her an idea. "Maybe I can make a 'Lost Puppy' poster," she suggested. "We could stick it all around the village with a photo of Pickle and our phone number. That way, more people will know he's missing and will help find him."

"That's a brilliant idea," Mum said. "If we design it on the computer, we can print off lots of copies."

"Can I do a poster too?" Jack asked. He'd been very quiet since Pickle had gone missing but seemed to brighten at Emily's suggestion. "I could use my paints."

Emily smiled. "Thanks, Jack," she said. "That would be really helpful."

Mum spread sheets of newspaper on the kitchen table and got out the paint and felt-tips for Jack while the computer whirred to life. Then Emily started work on her poster.

MISSING! she typed in big letters.

"Let's put in a big photo of Pickle so that everyone can see exactly what

he looks like," Mum said, opening up the folder of photos on the computer. "Why don't you choose one, and then I'll show you how to drop it into the document."

"OK," Emily agreed. A row of thumbnail photos appeared on screen and she clicked on the first to make it bigger. "Ohhh," she said, smiling. "Mum, look. Remember how tiny he was at first?"

Mum and Jack came to see. The photo

had been taken on the day Pickle had come to live with them, back when he was still so small that he could fit on Dad's hand. It showed him sitting on Emily's lap, his eyes wide and bright, and his head slightly cocked as if he were taking in his new surroundings. Both he and Emily looked really happy together.

"Adorable," Mum said. "Maybe for the poster you could find one of him when he's a bit older, though, to show what he looks like now?"

Emily scrolled through the photos. There was Pickle curled up fast asleep in his basket for the first time. He looked so teeny-tiny! Mind you, he hadn't slept for long that first night – he'd woken everyone up later on, crying piteously. "Poor thing, are you missing your mummy?" Emily had said when she went down to comfort him, stroking his trembling body.

Mum had appeared in the kitchen too, holding a small clock. She'd read that some little puppies liked sleeping with a ticking clock in their bed, because it reminded them of hearing their mother's heartbeat, so they tried it with Pickle . . . and within moments he'd fallen asleep, curled around the clock.

An hour later, though, the cries had come again. Emily crept downstairs a second time, taking him into her arms and cuddling him in the dark, quiet kitchen. "I'll look after you, Pickle, don't worry," she whispered to him. "I'll be your mummy now."

Once he'd dozed off, she'd slid him gently back into his basket and tiptoed up to her own bed . . . but then, at about five o'clock in the morning, she'd heard him *again*, making the saddest, loneliest little sounds. Unable to bear hearing him so miserable, she sneaked her pillow and a sleeping bag downstairs and spent the rest of the night dozing next to him on the kitchen floor.

Emily smiled, remembering how Mum had come in the next morning to find them both fast asleep. After that, Emily had been banned from sleeping on the kitchen floor – "You'll be too tired for school!" Mum had said – but they discovered that if Pickle went to bed with an alarm clock *and* a hot water bottle wrapped in a nice soft blanket, he slept much better. The warmth of the hot water bottle must have reminded him of sleeping with his mum and brothers and sisters, they thought.

Other photos in the collection showed Pickle getting used to living with them in different ways. One picture was of him all bedraggled and wet, after he'd fallen into his own water bowl. Another showed him falling asleep on Mum's fluffy pink slipper, and there were lots of him trotting about with his blue bear in his mouth. Then came the first day he was allowed outside – Emily would never forget that! Pickle had been so excited he must have sniffed every single blade of grass, and every leaf and flower in the garden!

"Have you found one yet?" Mum asked, interrupting Emily's memories.

"Not yet," she replied, flicking forward through more photos. Pickle with his new lead and collar. Pickle in the bath. Pickle playing with Jessie, Grandma's elderly Yorkshire terrier. Pickle in the park chasing after a football with Jack. There were so many lovely pictures, it was hard to choose one.

At last she found the perfect photo. It had been taken a week or so ago, when the whole family had gone out for a long walk together. The picture showed Pickle standing in a field, his tongue hanging out in a big smile. "This one would be good," she said, showing Mum.

"That's a lovely one," Mum agreed. "Oh yes – that was when we took a picnic on the Downs, wasn't it?"

"And Pickle rolled in the fox poo," Jack remembered with a laugh. "Yuck!"

Emily grinned. "Yes, and he pinched Dad's sandwich right out of his hand," she said. "Cheeky pup!"

Once Mum had shown Emily how to add the photo to the poster, Emily typed in a brief description of Pickle, and where he'd last been seen. Then she hesitated. "Do you think we should offer people a reward for finding him?" she wondered. "I've got six pounds in my money box."

"I've got two pounds fifty," Jack put in at once.

"That's very generous of you both," Mum said. "Keep your money, though. The reward can be that I'll make cakes for whoever finds Pickle — one cake a week for the next three months!"

Emily smiled. Mum was known throughout the village for her cakes. Nobody would be able to resist such a brilliant reward!

Free cake for three months to whoever finds Pickle, Emily typed, and added their phone number in a large, bold font. There! If that didn't get the whole village out searching for her puppy, nothing would.

"Finished!" Jack cried at that moment and held up his poster. There was a brown blobby picture of Pickle with four wonky legs, and underneath he'd written in careful black letters: *Pleese find our dogg Pickel. We miss himm so mutch.*

"I drew a sad face, too, to show that we're feeling sad," Jack said proudly.

"It's perfect," Emily said, giving her

MISSIN

OUR PUPPY
LAST SEEN
FREE CAKE
PHONE

PLeese find
our dogg Pickel
we miss himm
so mutch ☹

little brother a hug. "Thank you, Jack. Now *everybody* will know to look out for him."

"We'll take some photocopies at the village shop tomorrow morning, Jack," Mum said. "Then we can put them and Emily's poster all around the village."

Emily felt a bit better as copy after copy of her poster came rolling smoothly out from the printer. She'd done everything she could think of to find Pickle today. Tomorrow, the posters would go up, and she and Dad would set out searching in the fields and woods again. Someone would find him soon, she was sure of it. And whoever did would not only earn themselves lots of yummy cakes from Mum, but they'd have Emily's lifelong gratitude, too.

6

It was hard to get to sleep that night when all Emily could think about was Pickle. Eventually, after a lot of tossing and turning, she finally dozed off, only to dream that she was running through a forest calling her puppy's name. She kept thinking she saw his waggy white tail disappearing behind trees, and ran on and on through the undergrowth, calling breathlessly. *Wait for me, Pickle*, she kept shouting in the dream. *Stop!*

Emily woke with a start, her heart thudding. *It was just a dream*, she thought in relief – but then in the next moment, she remembered everything that had happened the day before. Pickle was still missing!

It was nearly six o'clock and she knew she wouldn't be able to sleep any more, so she scrambled out of bed and padded downstairs in her dressing gown. The kitchen seemed horribly silent without her friendly pup to greet her in his usual bouncy way.

She was just about to help herself to some cereal when the door opened, and in came Dad. "Couldn't sleep?" he said. "Me neither. Let's have a big breakfast, and then I'll make us some sandwiches and we can head off. We've got a Pickle-pup to bring home, haven't we?"

Emily smiled. She liked the way Dad seemed so certain that they'd find him. "We have," she agreed. "And we will!"

Dad put the kettle on and looked in the fridge. "All puppy-hunters should set off with a full stomach," he declared. "How does bacon, eggs and toast sound?"

"Perfect," Emily said happily. Dad's energy and enthusiasm was starting to rub off on her. *Yes, we* WILL *find Pickle today*, she thought to herself. *No doubt about it!*

Dad popped some slices of bread into the toaster while Emily poured them each some orange juice. Then she buttered the

toast while Dad cracked eggs into the hot frying pan and grilled the rashers of bacon.

After they'd eaten, Dad made a thermos of coffee and put together a picnic. "Hopefully we'll be back before lunch, but we might need provisions," he said. "Go and get dressed, Em, and brush your teeth while I have a quick shower. Then we'll get going."

By seven o'clock that morning, Dad and Emily were walking down the road. The sun had risen, painting the sky with streaks of apricot and rose, and the air felt cool and fresh. Jack was still asleep in bed but Mum had got up to wave them off. "Good luck," she'd said. "And let me know as soon as you have any news. Once Jack's up, we'll take the posters around the village and spread the word."

Dad had hesitated in the doorway with a grin. "About this reward. . ." he'd said cheekily. "If me and Em find Pickle, will we still get the cakes?"

Mum had laughed. "Absolutely," she'd replied. "With extra icing and sprinkles. I'll even make a special puppy-food cake for Pickle. See you later."

Emily and Dad headed into Albany Woods together. There was some early-morning mist clinging to the trees, which made it feel damp and spooky. "I hope Pickle didn't get too cold last night," Emily said, shoving her hands into her jacket pockets to keep them warm.

"I bet he squeezed himself into a cosy rabbit hole or badger sett," Dad said. "He's probably made friends with all the woodland animals by now."

Emily smiled. "Wouldn't it be great,"

she said, "if we were walking along, and Pickle's head suddenly popped up out of a rabbit hole?"

Dad laughed. "Now that I'd like to see," he agreed.

They walked right through the woods calling Pickle's name, but there was no sign of him. After a while, the mist cleared as the sun rose higher in the sky, and the birds began singing in the trees. *The perfect spring morning to walk your dog*, Emily thought to herself. Now they just needed to *find* their dog.

"Pickle!" she called in a high voice. "Piiiiiiickle!"

She wondered if Jack was awake yet and, if so, whether he and Mum had gone out to pin up posters around the village. With Pickle's picture on every lamp post and telegraph pole, he would

soon be the most famous dog in the neighbourhood.

Just then, Emily heard a faint sound on the breeze and stopped dead in her tracks. Barking. She could hear barking!

"PICKLE!" she shouted excitedly. The barking sounded just like her puppy . . . but where was he?

Woof! Woof! There it was again, so quiet you could only hear it if you strained to listen. "I think it's coming from this way," she said, pointing to her right. "Come on!"

She and Dad ran through the undergrowth, eyes scanning every single shrub and grassy patch. "Pickle, we're here!" she called again. "Pickle, we're coming!"

On and on they ran. Emily's heart was thumping with excitement. She couldn't believe they'd found Pickle already. She couldn't wait to scoop him up in the biggest cuddle ever!

WOOF! WOOF! The barking was getting louder. "Emily, I'm not completely sure. . ." Dad began saying just as they ran into a clearing. He broke off, and they both stopped running immediately.

"I'm not sure that *is* Pickle," Dad said quietly.

Emily's heart sank. There in front of them were two Border terriers excitedly bounding about together, with their owner coming up behind. One of the dogs barked again, and Emily felt a stab of disappointment as her excitement drained away. It had been these dogs that they'd heard, not Pickle. She'd been so certain it was him, too!

Dad put a hand on her shoulder while

he asked the terriers' owner if he'd seen a lost spaniel puppy. "Sorry, no," the man said. "But give me your number in case I do."

The man and his dogs went on their way. "Let's keep looking," Dad said.

Emily nodded, trying to stay positive. Pickle had to be *somewhere*, she reminded herself. And wherever he was, she would find him, even if it took her all day.

7

Emily and Dad searched through every
part of the woods, including around
the pond – although after his dunking
on Friday, Emily was pretty sure Pickle
would be more cautious about going
anywhere near that for a while! Once
they were confident that he definitely
wasn't in the woods, they went out into
the surrounding fields. Here, at least, the
land was flatter and it was easier to see
people and dogs from a distance, but they
made a point of walking up and down
all the hedgerows that edged the fields

just in case Pickle had fallen asleep or got stuck under one of them.

Next, they double-checked around the farms and asked the farm workers if they had seen Pickle. Nobody had, but everyone promised to keep an eye out. By now, Emily and Dad were hungry and thirsty after their early start, so they sat down to have a drink and a snack. While

Emily munched through a flapjack and a banana, Dad phoned Mum to see if she had any news.

"No sightings yet," he told Emily as he ended the call. "But Mum says she and Jack have put up posters all over the village. There's one on every street, and Mrs Abrahams at the shop has put one in her window, too. She's going to make sure all her customers see it, apparently."

Emily smiled. Mrs Abrahams was the nice kind of shop owner who'd often slip extra sweets into your bag with a wink, and on hot days she always left a bowl of water outside her shop so that passing dogs could have a drink. Suddenly Emily stiffened. "Dad – did you hear that?"

They both sat very still and listened. There it came again – a very faint barking.

Dad wrinkled his nose. "There are lots

of dogs out today, Em," he reminded her. "We can't get too excited every time we hear one."

"I know, but. . ." Emily paused, straining to listen again. Silence. "That did sound like Pickle."

"Em–" Dad said gently.

"I know, I know," she interrupted. "I said that last time and I was wrong. But this dog sounds more yappy, as if it's younger. Listen."

They both listened, but there was nothing to be heard now, just the low mooing of cattle in a field somewhere behind them. "Piiiiiickle!" Emily shouted at the top of her voice.

Yap. Yap-yap. "It's him," Emily said, jumping to her feet. "Dad, I know it's him. He must be somewhere around here."

Dad packed away the thermos flask

he'd been drinking from. "Try not to get your hopes up," he said. "It might not be him."

"I know," Emily replied. "But if it's somebody else's dog again, at least we can ask its owner if they've seen Pickle." The yapping came again. "I've just got a feeling it's him."

"Come on, then," Dad said, swinging the backpack on to his shoulders. "Follow that yap!"

They set off across the field, pausing every now and then to listen. "PICKLE!" Emily shouted.

Woof-woof! Yap-yap!

They were getting closer, she thought, quickening her step. And the closer they got, the surer she became that it was her dog.

"Pickle, we're coming!" she yelled.

Woof! Woof! "It's definitely him,"

she said, breaking into a run. "I don't understand why we can't see him, though. He sounds quite near now."

Dad jogged beside her. "Pickle!" he called.

WOOF! WOOF! Emily's heart tightened. She knew that was Pickle – she just knew it. They'd found him at last! But she still couldn't see him, even though the barking was so close.

"Sounds kind of echoey," Dad mused as they ran – and then all of a sudden he grabbed hold of Emily and held her tight. "Whoa!" he cried.

Emily gasped in alarm. There in front of them was a hole in the ground – a large hole about two metres across, as if the earth had just given way there. She stared in horror at the rocky walls of the hole. From where she was standing with

Dad, she couldn't tell how deep it was, but her legs felt wobbly just looking at it. Two more steps and she would have plunged straight down it. Was that what had happened to her poor little Pickle?

Woof-woof-woof, went the barking, impatiently now, as if to say, *Well, why have you stopped? I'm still here, you know!*

Dad was right. The barking *did* have an echo. "I think he must be down there," Dad said grimly. "Stay away from the edge, Em. We don't know how stable the ground is around here."

Emily bit her lip. She wanted to cheer with joy that they'd found Pickle – but how on earth were they going to get him out of the hole? And was he all right?

"How deep do you think it is?" she asked Dad, desperate to peer into the crater-like hole. She didn't dare go any closer to it in case the ground collapsed beneath her feet.

Dad lay down on his front and squirmed carefully towards the edge, moving just a few centimetres at a time. "Well, I can't see the bottom of it," he said, peering down. "It's too dark. Must be an old mineshaft or something – you do get them opening up from time to time. Actually, yes, I seem to remember hearing that there was a mine around here years ago. It must be from that. In a louder voice he called out "Pickle, are you there?" *There-there-there* went the echo.

Woof! Woof! came the excited response. "Oh fella," Dad said. "Have you been down there all night?" He reached back and pulled his phone out of his trouser pocket. Shuffling backwards so that he didn't risk dropping it into the hole, he pressed a button that made it work as a torch. Then he inched forward again and shone the bright beam of light downwards.

"Yep, I can see him," he said, peering into the gloom. "Hello, mate. Hello!"

Pickle barked joyfully. It was absolutely the best sound in the world, Emily thought. "I'm here too, Pickle," she called happily. "I promise we'll rescue you!"

"He's standing up wagging his tail, so hopefully that means he hasn't broken any bones," Dad went on. "Good boy, you wait there. We'll find a way to get you out, don't worry."

He shuffled back again and stood up, and then he and Emily hugged each other. "I'm so glad we've found him," Emily said, tears of relief pricking her eyes. "I can't believe he's down there, though. Poor thing — what a shock it must have been for him: running along cheerfully only to suddenly fall into an enormous hole!"

"No wonder we couldn't see him," Dad said. "And it's a miracle he seems OK."

He shook his head. "Typical Pickle. He can't even get lost in a boring, sensible way, can he? He's got to turn it into a crazy adventure."

Emily grinned. She felt so so happy that they'd found her puppy she could hardly put the feeling into words. "Let's tell Mum the news," she suggested.

"Good idea," Dad said, dialling home. "We claim the cake!" he cried when Mum answered.

Mum's reply was so high-pitched with excitement that Emily could hear every word. "You found him?"

"We did, although he's a bit stuck right now. . ."

Dad went on to explain the situation while Emily sat as near to the edge of the hole as she dared and talked to Pickle, telling him all the lovely things they would do together just as soon as he was out.

Woof, went Pickle eagerly as soon as she mentioned the word "squirrel".

After speaking to Mum, Dad phoned the RSPCA, a charity who rescued animals in trouble and also had vets who could care for ill or injured creatures. The person he spoke to suggested contacting the local fire station, too, as specialist equipment might be needed for the rescue.

"Don't worry, Pickle," Emily called. "The rescue team are on their way!"

8

Dad sat with Emily by the hole while they waited for help to arrive. The nearest road was the farm track at the edge of the field, and after about twenty minutes or so, the Fire and Rescue Service truck arrived, quickly followed by an RSPCA vehicle.

"Here they are," Dad said, as two fire officers got out of the truck and came walking over towards them. "Hopefully they'll have a ladder that's long enough to reach down there."

Emily smiled. "Did you hear that, boy?" she called. "Not much longer in the hole. We'll soon have you out."

A low woof greeted her words.

"Hello there," said the first fire officer as he and his colleague arrived on the scene. He was a tall, sandy-haired man with lots of freckles. When he saw the hole in the ground he gave a low whistle. "Goodness me. Well, that's definitely a disused mineshaft. A big one, too, by the looks of things. Once we've got your dog out we'll have to find out who owns the land here and get them to cap it off." Seeing Emily's blank gaze, he added,

"That means we'll cover it over with some strong mesh so that nobody else can fall down it."

"But before that," said the second fire officer, who was a woman with short dark hair and blue eyes, "we'd better see about getting your poor little puppy out, hadn't we?"

"Yes, please," said Emily.

Woof! went Pickle, as if he could understand every word. *Yes, please, and can you hurry up about it? I've got squirrels to chase, not to mention my Emily to lick,* Emily imagined him saying.

The officers from the RSPCA team drove across the field and parked nearby. Two men got out wearing smart, navy blue and white uniforms. "Hi, guys," said the first. "What's the story here, then? We've been told there's a six-month-old

spaniel puppy who's down the hole, is that right?"

"That about sums it up," Dad replied.

The first RSPCA man opened the back doors of their 4 x 4. "I'm Gary," he said, "and this is Alex. We've brought some kit with us to help with the rescue."

"That way we can treat your dog as soon as we get him out," added Alex.

The fire officers talked in low voices

together, and then the sandy-haired man did what Dad had done – he lay on his front to safely examine the hole. He ran his hands around the top of the hole, sending a small shower of soil tumbling down. Pickle gave a surprised yelp below.

"Sorry, pal," the man said. He stood up again and shook his head. "I don't like the look of this," he said. "I reckon it's at least ten metres deep, and even a preliminary look tells me that it's unstable. I can't risk myself or Jen here going down, I'm afraid – or anyone else. We could end up injuring ourselves or sending a rockfall on to the dog."

Emily felt dismayed. This was not what she'd wanted to hear. Not at all! "So . . . how *are* we going to get him out?" she asked nervously. "We can't just leave him down there."

Alex gave her a reassuring smile. "Don't worry, there are other things we can try," he said. "We can send down a Vari Kennel on a harness and see if he'll climb into it."

"A what?" Emily asked. "A kennel?"

"A Vari Kennel," Alex repeated. "It's a pet carrier. If we lower it down with the door open, with a bit of luck, he might climb inside. And then—"

"You can pull him up, like a bucket from a well!" Emily finished. She smiled, imagining Pickle's happy face peeping out as he rose to the surface.

"Exactly," Gary said.

"So how will this harness work, then?" Dad asked. "Have either of you got a winch?"

Jen, the fire officer, took out some keys from her pocket. "One winch coming right up," she said. "I'll just grab it from the truck."

"And we've got a harness and Vari Kennel that'll be the perfect size for your dog," Alex said, before heading towards the van. "Let's do it!"

It was all starting to feel rather exciting, Emily thought as the rescue team sprang into action. The winch Jen brought back looked like a canister, with steel rope wound around a central spool and a solid metal base that would keep it firmly on the ground. There was a large hook on the end of the rope, and Alex attached it securely to the harness. The harness was made up of four metal chains, which he and Gary clipped tightly to the sturdy plastic kennel.

"Ready?" Jen asked.

"Ready," Gary replied, positioning the kennel so that it dangled over the hole.

Jen pressed a button and a motor inside the winch began to whirr. Then the cable started spooling out, lowering the harness and kennel into the mineshaft.

"Cool," said Emily. She felt giddy at the thought of Pickle being hoisted back up again in the pet carrier. It would be like a ride at a doggy funfair for him!

Gary lay down and shone a torch into the hole. "Keep going," he instructed as

the kennel vanished into the shaft. "Keep going. And . . . stop. It's at the bottom now."

Jen turned off the motor and the cable was still.

"Good lad," Gary called down encouragingly to Pickle. "He's sniffing the kennel," he told the others. "Go on, boy, that's it, in you get."

Silence fell as they waited hopefully for Pickle to do what he was told. Emily realized she was holding her breath. "Go on, Pickle," she called, imagining his puzzled face. *What is this they've sent down?* he was probably wondering. "Climb in, Pickle, good boy," she urged.

A few moments passed. "Hmm," said Gary, still shining the torchlight down. "He's not having it, I'm afraid. He's just backing away looking confused."

Emily sighed but Dad squeezed her hand. "I imagine he's still a bit jittery after the shock of falling," he said. "Perhaps he doesn't understand what we're trying to do."

"He's most likely scared," Alex agreed. "Animals often panic when they're stuck like this."

"The kennel probably smells of other animals, too," Gary added. "Go on, boy, get in. There's nothing to worry about."

"Come on, Pickle, it's OK," Emily called. They had to make this work, she thought desperately. Pickle *had* to get in the kennel, there was no other way out!

"Nope," Gary said after a while. "He's still backing away from it, looking very wary. Let's give him another minute or so, and then we'll try something else."

"Could we tempt him up here with

food?" Emily suggested. "He knows the sound of the puppy-food box when you shake it. He might work out that we're trying to rescue him if he hears it."

"It's worth a try," Alex said. "He must be pretty hungry by now."

Gary edged back from the hole and stood up, brushing himself down. "We can also try sending down some things from home that he's familiar with," he added. "Anything that smells of home will make him feel safer."

"We could send down your slippers, Dad," Emily suggested. "He loves playing with those."

"So he does," Dad said. "Well, we can give it a shot." He got his phone out again. "I'll call Mum and ask her to bring them along with the box of puppy food."

"And his cuddly bear," Emily added.

"The one he sleeps with every night. That might cheer him up."

It felt good to be doing something helpful, she thought as Dad phoned Mum. Emily might not have a winch and harness to rescue her dog, but she was Pickle's best friend, and knew him better than anyone. Surely some breakfast and his favourite bear would be enough to tempt Pickle into the kennel and up to safety. Wouldn't it?

9

Jen the fire officer pressed the button to haul up the kennel. The motor whirred and the spool began to rotate anticlockwise, winding the cable neatly back on to the drum. Once it had reached the surface, Alex lifted the kennel over the edge of the mineshaft and set it back on the ground.

Dad passed around a packet of biscuits while they waited for Mum and Jack to arrive. Emily heard Pickle give a little whine as if he could smell the food. *Poor thing*, she thought. *He must be so hungry and thirsty down there.* He was normally ravenous at breakfast time every morning – and now he hadn't eaten or drunk anything for over twenty-four hours.

After about ten minutes, they saw the family's blue car pull up behind the fire truck, and Mum and Jack emerge. Jack had a huge smile on his face as they approached. "You found him!" he cried happily. "Pickle, it's me, Jack!

Pickle woofed in reply.

Mum was carrying a large bag on her shoulder. She grabbed Jack's hand as they neared the hole. She hugged Dad and Emily, then turned pale as she saw the mineshaft. "My goodness," she said, her hand flying up to her mouth. "I can't believe it. Is he really down there? It's a miracle he even—"

She broke off quickly, glancing at Jack, but Emily could guess what she'd been about to say – that it was a miracle Pickle had even survived after such a fall. Emily couldn't bear to think that way. Changing the subject, she asked, "Did you bring the things we asked for, Mum?"

Mum gathered herself. "Yes," she said, taking the bag off her shoulder. It was the one they sometimes used for picnics. She reached inside. "I've brought along Pickle's food, some of his toys, and Dad's slippers. Oh, and the blanket from his basket, too. I've been meaning to wash that all week because it's a bit smelly – I'm glad I didn't."

"Smelly is good in this instance," Alex said with a grin. "So, let's give this a try. How about we tip some of the food into

our kennel and put in his toy as well.
That ought to reassure him that it's OK
to clamber aboard."

"Maybe a slipper, too," Emily suggested.
"He was playing with those yesterday
morning. He really loves them."

"Okey-doke," said Alex.

Emily shook the box of puppy food
so that Pickle could hear it and tipped a
handful into the bottom of the kennel.

Then she added his cuddly bear and the slipper with chew marks on it for good measure.

"OK, guys, second time lucky," said Pete, the sandy-haired fire officer. He noticed Jack staring wide-eyed at the winch and beckoned him over. "Want to press the special button, buddy?"

"Yes, *please*," Jack said at once. Pete showed him what to do and Jack solemnly pressed the switch to start the winch's motor.

With Gary shining the torch and Alex guiding the cable, the kennel was gently lowered down, down, down into the hole once more. "Let's hope this works," Mum said.

"Of course it will," Dad replied. "Like anyone's been able to resist the smell of my feet before!"

Emily barely heard them. She could hardly stand the anticipation.

"All right . . . we're down," Gary said after a few moments. "Stop the winch."

Pete stopped the motor and once again, everyone fell silent while they waited. Would Pickle trust the kennel enough to step inside now?

"That's it, boy," Gary called coaxingly. "Smells good, huh? That's your breakfast, that is. Go on, try a bit."

Emily was crossing her fingers so tightly that her knuckles had turned white. *Come on, Pickle*, she urged in her head. *I know this must be a bit weird and scary but it'll be OK – I promise!*

Gary sucked in a breath and Emily leaned forward. "He's sniffing the food," Gary reported in a low voice. "Yep, he's moving towards it, he. . ." Then he broke off.

"What? What's happening?" Emily asked anxiously.

"He's not daft, your dog, is he?" Gary said with a sigh in his voice. "He still doesn't quite trust us. He's standing there with just his head in the kennel, leaning forward to get the food. He's too suspicious to step right into it."

"We could try lifting the kennel a tiny way off the ground," Alex suggested. "See if he decides to scramble in fully so that he can keep eating. He's obviously hungry."

"Let's try," Gary agreed. "Could we go up a few centimetres, please?"

Pete pressed the button to start the motor on the winch, and almost immediately turned it off again.

Gary shook his head. "Nope," he said. "Now he's backed away again. Drop it back down, please."

Alex turned to Emily. "Maybe if you encourage him," he suggested. "Call down to him."

Emily nodded. "Pickle, where's the slipper?" she called. "Where's the slipper, Pickle?"

They heard a faint woof in reply.

"He knows your voice," Gary said. "He's looking up the side of the shaft, trying to see you."

"Find the slipper, Pickle! Where is it?" Emily called again.

"I don't think he understands," Gary said, and Emily's heart sank. Oh no! She had been so sure that the scent of Dad's slipper and the cuddly toy would make her puppy realize that the little kennel was safe. He wasn't usually a shy or nervous kind of dog, but he obviously felt confused by this strange situation and didn't know what to do. She could see why. If *she'd* fallen down a hole, she might be in two minds about climbing into a strange box that kept moving up and down, too.

"Go on, boy," she tried again. "Get in the kennel, it's fine!"

The words seemed to echo around her head, reminding her of how she'd been teaching Pickle to get into his basket with a similar command. Wait. . . Maybe that was it?

"I wonder if. . ." she began, then stopped. Her thoughts were spinning around so fast it took her a moment to form them into proper sentences. "I was just thinking, I've been teaching Pickle to get into his basket at home," she said, the words tumbling out. "If we made the Vari Kennel look a bit like his basket – you know, by putting in his blanket and the toy – and then I shout, 'Get in your basket!', he might understand and get in."

Gary and Alex looked at each other. "Not a bad idea," Alex said. "Let's haul this up again and try it."

"Or, even better," Mum said, "we could send down his actual basket. It's not very big – it should fit in the kennel." She smiled at Emily. "I brought it in the car in case he wanted to cuddle up in it on the way home."

Emily hugged Mum. "Brilliant! Shall I go and get it?"

"I will," said Mum. "I think you're needed here with Pickle."

★

Mum hurried back to the car while the kennel was smoothly winched up to the surface again.

"What's he doing now?" Emily asked Gary, who was still peering into the shaft.

"He's lying down with his head on his front paws, looking a bit sorry for himself," Gary replied. "Hey, don't give up, boy. We'll get you out," he called down in a kind voice.

Emily glanced over at Mum, who was now running back towards them with Pickle's basket in her arms. "Here she comes," she said. Emily had butterflies in her tummy. She really hoped this new idea worked.

Mum and Emily set up Pickle's basket just the way he liked it, with the snuggly blanket covering the base and his cuddly toy at the side. Then they tucked it into the

kennel. It was a perfect fit, thank goodness.

"*Third* time lucky," Pete said when they were ready. "Can you press the button for me again, please, Jack?"

Jack didn't hesitate to do as he was asked, and once again the motor whirred and out spooled the rope.

The kennel disappeared from view and Emily crossed all the fingers she could possibly cross. She desperately hoped Pickle would know what to do this time!

10

"And . . . we're down," Gary said. "Thank you!"

Pete stopped the winch and they all waited again. "Get in your basket, Pickle," Emily called. "Good boy, get in your basket!"

"He's sniffing at it," Gary said. "Try calling again."

"Can I lie down like Gary?" Emily asked her parents. "Please? I won't do anything silly. Maybe if Pickle can see me, that would help."

"OK," Mum decided. "I'll hang

on to your ankles, though. Just for my peace of mind."

Emily got down on her front and edged closer to the mineshaft. She peeped over the edge and followed Gary's torchlight to see Pickle right down at the bottom of the hole, cautiously sniffing his basket inside the kennel.

A little cry escaped her throat at the sight of him. He looked so far away and so tiny down there. "Hey, you," she called down. "Hello, Pickle."

Pickle looked up – and barked excitedly to see her face. His feathery tail whisked back and forth at great speed.

"Yes, it's me," she said smiling. "I'm all the way up here!" She took a deep breath, hoping she hadn't made her puppy too excited to listen properly. "Now, Pickle. I need you to be really clever for me. Can you get in your basket, Pickle? Get in your basket!"

He looked at the basket and back up at Emily. Even through the gloom, she could see a questioning look in his eyes, as if he were saying, *Are you sure? You seriously want me to get in that?*

"He understood you," Gary said. "He's

definitely thinking about it. Try sounding really confident about it this time. Don't ask him − tell him."

Emily nodded. She was starting to feel a bit light-headed from peering into the mineshaft and was very glad to have Mum still holding tightly on to her. It was a long, long way down. "Get in your basket, Pickle!" she said in the sing-song voice she used for commands. She made herself sound as confident as she could. "Get in your basket!"

Pickle gave a little woof and then put his front paws in the basket. "Good boy," Emily called. "*Clever* boy. Get in your basket, that's it. In your basket!"

She could hardly breathe with excitement as, with one last look up at his mistress, Pickle gingerly stepped into the Vari kennel.

"Good boy! Now sit! Sit down! And stay!" Emily's heart thumped. She was half expecting Pickle to jump straight out of the basket, as he'd done so many times before, but to her amazement, he stayed inside. She could just about see him turning around in there as if he was making himself comfortable.

"We've got him," Gary said softly, and patted Emily on the back. "Well done, love. Right, let's haul him up, nice and slow. We mustn't frighten him now."

Pete pressed the button on the winch and the kennel jerked slightly as the harness tightened to take Pickle's weight. "Good boy," Emily called encouragingly. "Stay there, Pickle. Stay!"

The time it took for the kennel to be hoisted slowly back up to the surface felt like the longest moments of Emily's life. She was terrified Pickle might take fright and leap out of the basket again, so she kept a steady stream of encouraging chatter as gradually, gradually, the kennel rose up and up. "You're so clever," she told him. "What a good boy. What a clever boy to sit and stay in the basket!"

The kennel drew closer and closer and now Pickle's little face was clearly visible as he looked out of the kennel door, still sitting in the basket. As soon as he saw Emily he gave a loud woof and his eyes shone with happiness. "We mustn't let him jump towards you," Alex warned as it came almost to the surface. "The big worry is that he'll jump out again and hurt himself. We need him to sit tight until we've got him all the way up. Stay there, Pickle. Good boy!"

Pickle blinked as he saw daylight but remained sitting safely in the basket. "Nearly there," Emily said happily. "Stay, Pickle. Good boy!"

Pickle woofed softly. Through the holes in the side of the kennel, Emily saw his tail wagging.

Finally, the winch had brought the

kennel all the way up to the top of the hole, and Alex was able to guide it carefully to the surface. Emily and Gary wriggled back from the edge of the mineshaft while Alex unclipped the kennel from the harness. Then he lifted it a safe distance from the mineshaft and set it gently down on the ground.

"Pickle!" Emily cried, putting her hand inside the kennel to pat him. He licked her fingers, then clambered shakily out. Emily rested her head on his dusty fur and hugged him, while he wagged his tail faster than ever. "Oh, Pickle," she said again, a huge lump in her throat. "I missed you!"

"Well done, everyone," said Pete behind her. "Fantastic teamwork! Jen, let's get some fencing around this hole, quick, to stop anyone else having an accident."

Jack, Mum and Dad crowded around
Emily and Pickle, all trying to pat him
and stroke him at once. Mum had tears
in her eyes.

"Aww." Gary laughed. "I love a happy
ending. Well done, Emily – you did great.
Now, we'd better check Pickle over to make
sure he's OK. He should definitely see a vet
later to give him a proper examination,

but we'll do what we can here."

"Let's give him some water, too," Alex said, pouring some into a bowl. "He must be dehydrated by now."

As soon as Alex set the bowl of water down on the grass for him, Pickle bent to have a long splashy drink. While he drank, Gary checked his pulse and breathing, then gently felt his legs and back.

"He's still shivering," Alex noticed. "Let's get a nice warm blanket around you, fella."

"I can't detect any obvious breaks," Gary said as Alex went to fetch a blanket, "and he's moving OK. Bit of grazing on his front paws here and a few bumps and bruises." He lifted Pickle's head, gently opened his mouth and pressed a finger on his gum for a few seconds. Then he took his finger away and nodded. "Yep –

the gums are pale and not regaining their colour. He's in shock," he said. "Hardly surprising."

Alex draped a thick red blanket around Pickle and patted him. "There you are. We'll soon have you warmed up, boy."

"His heartbeat's rather fast," Gary went on, "although again, that's understandable. His breathing sounds clear, though."

Emily grinned. "But he's all right? After that gigantic fall? I can't believe it!"

"He's a miracle pup." Mum laughed. "Tough as old boots, aren't you, Pickle?"

"Like I said, he should be looked over properly by a vet today," Gary said. "He almost certainly needs some painkillers and probably needs those grazes bandaging, too. But generally speaking, he'll be fine." He scratched Pickle behind the ears.

Emily saw Mum and Dad exchange a look. "Hmm," said Mum. "I'm pretty sure our vet is closed on Sundays."

"Do you know if there are any around here that might be open?" Dad asked.

"Well, of course there's the RSPCA centre down the road," Gary replied. "They have a clinic that is definitely open – I reckon that's your best bet."

"Thanks," said Dad. "I know where it is. We'll take him over there now."

Emily thanked the fire officers, who were putting up some temporary metal fences with large warning signs around the hole. "Our pleasure," Jen told her. "I'm glad your puppy's going to be OK."

"Me too," Emily said. Then she carefully lifted Pickle back into his basket, which was still in the kennel, and Gary showed her how to fasten the door.

"Just leave the Vari Kennel and the blanket at the RSPCA centre when you've finished with them," he told her.

"Thanks for everything," Dad said to Alex and Gary as they packed their equipment back into the 4 x 4.

"Yes, thank you," Emily said. "From me *and* Pickle."

Alex grinned. "Glad to help," he said.

The journey to the RSPCA centre didn't take long and, once there, Dad carried the kennel to the reception area, with Emily, Mum and Jack close behind.

"Hello, how can I help?" asked the receptionist behind the desk.

Dad explained the situation, and Emily chipped in with extra details. Now that Pickle was safely by her side, the enormity of what had happened was just starting to hit her. She started to feel quite upset as they explained to the receptionist how they'd had to rescue her puppy after his fall.

"My goodness!" cried the receptionist. "You *have* been through it, haven't you? What a story. Have a seat in the waiting area and I'll get one of our vets to look at Pickle as soon as possible, OK?"

"Thanks," Emily said.

Mum put her arm around her as they sat and waited. "Are you all right?" she asked.

Emily nodded. It was hard to explain how she felt. It was as if she'd kept herself going and going for all this time, with hardly a chance to think straight. All of a sudden, now that she could stop worrying so much, she felt as if someone had deflated her and let all of her energy leak away.

Pickle gave a low whine in the dog carrier as he saw a cat in a basket nearby. The cat hissed and fluffed up its fur in reply.

"It's all right, Pickle-pops," Emily soothed. "Take no notice."

Thankfully, they didn't have to wait long to see the vet. Her name was Ayesha, and she had long dark hair in a ponytail. "Let's have a look at this daredevil pup," she said with a smile.

Pickle seemed nervous at being in the vet's room. His eyes were big and anxious as he stared around, and his ears went down when Ayesha carefully lifted him on to her table. "Hello, Pickle, don't worry," she said in a soft voice. "I know there are some strange smells in here, from other animals who've been in before you, but I promise you're safe with me."

Emily reached out to stroke him as he made a small whining sound in the back of his throat. "Good boy," she told him.

Ayesha checked him all over very thoroughly. She gave him a painkilling injection, which she said would make him feel better very quickly, and a first dose of antibiotics. Then she cleaned the grazes on his front legs, dabbed in some antiseptic cream and wound bandages around them, then swabbed at one of his paws where it looked sore.

"The good news is, he's going to be absolutely fine," she said after a while. "No broken bones and no serious damage. He might feel a bit tender for a few days, so he should take it easy, and you'll need to finish the course of antibiotics, just to make sure those grazes

don't get infected." She smiled and gave
Pickle a friendly pat. "Other than that,
he'll be back to his usual self in no
time."

"Thank you," Emily said happily, giving
Pickle a hug. She quite wanted to hug
Ayesha too, but managed to stop herself.

Dad laughed. "Back to his usual self?"
he said, ruffling Pickle's fur. "I'd better
hide my slippers, then – not to mention

all the other shoes. First things first, though. Let's go home."

WOOF!, went Pickle, sounding as if he thoroughly agreed, and everyone laughed.

11

Pickle was so exhausted after his adventures that he slept on Emily's lap all the way home in the car. Emily, meanwhile, couldn't stop smiling.

Once they were back, she unclipped her seatbelt carefully and scooped up her dozing puppy to carry him inside. It felt as if they had been away for ages.

"Oh Emily, you're back! And there's Pickle!" came two voices just then. She looked up to see Mr and Mrs Turner hurrying over with big smiles on their faces. "Is he OK? We heard he'd taken a tumble and got stuck down a hole, poor little thing!"

"He's fine, thanks," Dad replied. "A bit bumped and bruised, but nothing that a few days' rest won't sort out, we hope."

"Rest? Pickle?" Mr Turner chuckled, his eyes twinkling. "That'll be a first."

"Oh, I *am* pleased," Mrs Turner said. "What a scare!"

Pickle opened his eyes at all the voices and gave a sleepy little woof. Then he licked Emily's face for the hundredth time, just because he could.

"Is that Pickle? You found him!" came another voice, and there was Mrs Jackson, walking Buster along the lane. "What happened? Where was he?"

And then, just as Emily had finished explaining, along came Mr Warburton with his dog, Sammy, who made a fuss of Pickle, too.

"I feel like I'm friends with a film star or something," Emily laughed, once she'd told the story again. "All this attention you're getting from everyone, Pickle. Next, you'll be signing autographs with your paws!"

"Paw-tographs," Dad quipped with a grin.

"Let's get this famous pooch inside, anyway," Mum said. "Inside – and straight to bed. He's got a lot of sleep to catch up on."

Emily carried Pickle inside and tucked him cosily into his basket in the kitchen. As soon as he was comfortable, he fell fast asleep all over again. Emily curled up next to him, listening to him breathing. She'd never been so pleased and happy to be home before. What's more, the house *felt* like home again, now that Pickle was back.

While Pickle slept, Emily drew a chart of when he had to have his next antibiotics so that they wouldn't forget, then helped Mum make a special cake for her family of intrepid animal-rescuers. Meanwhile, Dad and Jack went around the village, taking down their lost-puppy posters, grateful that they were no longer needed.

Chloe and her mum popped in later with a doggy treat for Pickle, and a couple of other friends phoned up to say how pleased they were that he was all right. Even the local radio station had got hold of the story and rang, wanting an interview.

Pickle slept through the whole thing.

Every now and then he would open his
eyes blearily, see Emily and his cuddly
bear, and then give a little sigh of
contentment and fall straight back asleep.

"Bless him, he's worn out," Mum said.
"Too tired even to be cheeky."

Emily grinned. "Ah, just you wait," she
said, stroking him gently. "Pickle won't
be quiet for long. In a few days, he'll

be bouncing about, as daft as ever." She buried her nose in his soft brown fur and breathed in the smell of him. "And we'll have lots and lots of fun together again, won't we, boy?"

Pickle thumped his tail sleepily in reply, and Emily smiled. Her best friend was home, and that was all that mattered. She couldn't wait for their next adventure together. But one thing was for sure – from now on, all adventures would *definitely* be above ground!

Meet A Real RSPCA Inspector – Gary Eastwood

Although the characters you've just read about are fictional, Pickle's story is based on a rescue that really did happen. In real life, it was a dog, not a puppy, that fell down the mineshaft, and that dog's name was Bean. Inspector Gary Eastwood was part of the rescue team.

Photo by Inspector Gary Eastwood

Bean after the rescue

Tell us about the rescue you were a part of.

Bean's owners had been on a camping trip when Bean disappeared. They contacted the RSPCA, and I was the Inspector on call. I was worried about how we were going to pull Bean out of the mineshaft safely, and I came up with the idea of lowering a long crate into the shaft using two ropes. I realized that if we encouraged Bean into the crate, then tilted it and pulled it up using one rope, the dog would be unable to jump out and hurt himself more.

We tried lots of things to get Bean into the basket – old socks and dog food – but it was only when we put in his blanket and told Bean to "get in his basket" that Bean actually did – just like Pickle!

What was the trickiest part of the rescue?

The trickiest part of the rescue was working

out how we were going to lower something down to Bean and what equipment we needed. I am especially proud of this rescue, as I thought of how to lower something down for Bean to jump into.

Why did you want to become an RSPCA Inspector?

I became an RSPCA officer by accident! I was unemployed and on the bus one day in Leeds, on the way to do some voluntary work. I missed my stop and got off outside the Leeds branch of the RSPCA. I heard lots of dogs barking and went to investigate.

Noticing the RSPCA building, I banged on the door and the centre manager came to answer it. I was invited in for a tour and ended up volunteering for the RSPCA and working at the centre. A little bit later, one of the RSPCA staff suggested that I apply to be an Inspector – so I did and the rest is history!

Could you describe what a typical day is like for an RSPCA Inspector?

A lot of my time is spent on housing estates following up calls from members of the public concerned about an animal and how it is being cared for. Sometimes this means catching an abandoned animal, or helping one that isn't being looked after properly.

Occasionally I get involved in a more exciting rescue like Bean's. Today, for instance, I helped out with the rescue of a young calf that had strayed on to a main road through a hole in the hedge. I had to help guide the calf back through the hole into the field and then help patch the hole up!

What is the best thing about being an RPSCA Inspector?

The best thing about being an inspector is helping an animal out of a sticky situation and seeing it healthy and happy again and in a loving home.

What To Do if Your Dog Goes Missing

 If your dog goes missing, get an adult to contact your local police station to ask if a dog like yours has been found.

 Your milkman and postman may also be able to help you by looking out for your dog on their rounds.

It's a good idea to put up a poster in your local area with a picture of your dog, for example in newsagents and schools. You need permission to put posters up, so make sure you ask first – even if it's just a lamp post, you need to ask the council.

 Local newspapers may have a section for advertising lost pets – you could even ask your local radio to make an announcement.

Five Tips: Training a Puppy

 Start training your puppy from an early age.

 If your puppy obeys you, reward him or her with a treat. Your puppy will quickly learn that nice things happen when he or she pleases you!

 Only use positive, reward-based training.

 Never shout at or punish your puppy.

 Always make sure that treats are appropriate for a puppy's diet. You should only give treats that are designed especially for dogs. If your puppy receives treats through training, you may need to adjust the amount of food in his or her food bowl.

Collect the whole series...

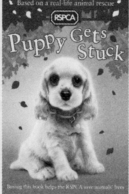

Coming in
May 2013

Coming in
October 2013

You'll also love...

Packed with cute stickers and fun facts!